Chicken

PIES

for the

Soul

Grade-A PARODY

by Jay Forman
Inspired by the animated film *Chicken Run*
Screenplay by Karey Kirkpatrick
Story by Peter Lord and Nick Park
Directed by Peter Lord and Nick Park
Produced by Peter Lord, David Sproxton, and Nick Park

Aardman™

DREAMWORKS™

PATHÉ!™

Dedication

This book is dedicated to chickens everywhere who, cooped up against their will, lead lives of quiet desperation....You know who you are.
May you find the courage to follow your dreams!

PUFFIN BOOKS
Published by the Penguin Group
Penguin Putnam Books for Young Readers,
345 Hudson Street, New York, New York 10014, U.S.A.
Penguin Books Ltd, 27 Wrights Lane, London W8 5TZ, England
Penguin Books Australia Ltd, Ringwood, Victoria, Australia
Penguin Books Canada Ltd, 10 Alcorn Avenue, Toronto, Ontario, Canada M4V 3B2
Penguin Books (N.Z.) Ltd, 182-190 Wairau Road, Auckland 10, New Zealand

Penguin Books Ltd, Registered Offices: Harmondsworth, Middlesex, England

Published by Puffin Books,
a division of Penguin Putnam Books for Young Readers, 2000

Puffin Books ISBN 0-14-130877-X

Printed in the United States of America

Chicken Pies for the Soul

Contents

Section Three

Section Four

MRS TWEEDY'S CHICKEN PIES

Ginger's Acknowledgments

—as dictated to Babs

"First off I would like to thank Bunty, whose prodigious egg-laying bought us the time we needed to plan a proper escape. And it seems that she is about to become a mother . . . again! That makes it, let's see . . . eight?"

"Seventeen."

"*Seventeen?*"

"Well chuffed I am with that. Well chuffed, indeed!"

"Well, Bunty, *someone* must be full of more than just hot air. Anyhow, Nick and Fetcher negotiated the contract for the manuscript, so I suppose we owe them some recognition."

"And eggs. That's in the fine print there, it is."

"Yes, thank you, Nick. I'm sure we'll find *many* items in the small print over time. Babs knitted the design elements. . . ."

"Are we going off on holiday, then? You promised that when we finished the book we would take a lovely holiday down by—"

"Just wait a moment, Babs, I'm not quite done here.

Thanks also to Fowler, and apologies as well, as we *simply* couldn't find room for all 239 pages of his reminiscences."

"Hmmph!"

"Yes, Fowler, it is the reader's loss I am sure. And finally a special heartfelt thanks goes out to the wonderful folks at DreamWorks and Penguin Putnam. . . ."

"Penguins? I thought it was about chickens!"

"No, Babs, we're the chickens. Penguin Putnam is the name of the publishing company that made this book possible."

"Are we done here, doll face? I've got a meeting at three o'clock and I don't want to be late. I'm gonna learn how to drive stick."

"Yes, Rocky, we're done."

"Yeehaw! Look out L.A.—there's a new rooster in town, and *this* one goes from 0 to 60 in 5.9 flat!"

"You roosters are all the same."

"You said it, doll face. Let's scramble!"

"Oh dear, did he say scramble?"

"It's okay, Babs. It's just a figure of speech."

Introduction

Dear Readers,

Not too long ago we were prisoners on a gloomy farm, forced to lay eggs for a living. If we failed, we would end up in the pot. Fences surrounded us, dogs barked at us, and dull-witted Mr. Farmer shadowed our every movement. It was a wretched existence, and we often despaired. Yet buried in the heart of even the fattest and most timid hen lies a seed of courage and determination—a seed that needs only the sunlight of inspiration and the water of encouragement to bear fruit. We found such things in the hour of our greatest need, and they gave us the strength to change our lives. We went from being passive egg-layers to bold risk-takers, we joined together as a team, which enabled us to escape from the farm and fly to the promised land. After we arrived, we agreed to set pen to paper and recount the stories and lessons that gave us the conviction to "seize the day." This book is the fruit of our labor; it is our Golden Egg.

Inside you will find many tales, some funny, others touching, and (hopefully) all enlightening in some way or another. It is our hope that they will give you guidance in your times of trial, encouragement in your moments of doubt, and bring levity when all else seems tepid and dull. We have tried to cover many points of view, from roosters to rats to farmers, in the hopes that we may touch everybody in some way. So read on and enjoy; you may never look at chickens quite the same way again.

Sincerely,

Ginger & Company
(I knitted the design!—anonymous)

"Over in America, we have this rule. If you wanna motivate someone—Don't—mention—DEATH!" —Rocky

THAT WHICH DOES NOT PLUCK YOU MAKES YOU STRONGER:

Overcoming Obstacles and Living Your Dream

How to Boost an Ego

"Let's rock 'n' roll." — ROCKY

When I first dropped in—I mean, *landed*—on Tweedy's Farm, I noticed right away that most of the gals lacked confidence. Sure, they were swell chicks and all, but a lot of them just didn't *believe* in themselves. Granted, the threat of being chopped up for dinner didn't help much, but this group was deep in the dumps at one point. And that was Ginger's fault; she was so busy scaring them she never took the time to see what a good job she was doing. Ginger had some funny ideas concerning motivation. She wasn't exactly Miss Sunshine on the Daisies, if you catch my drift. Her inspirational techniques left a lot to be desired. Threatening the troops with Certain Death in the case of failure does not exactly improve morale. It is true that she really wanted to help the girls out, but her demanding (and unsuccessful) schemes often ended up eating away at the gang's confidence rather than beefing it up.

Now ego is something the Rock has in abundance, which is good because it seems to be in short supply over here in England. Americans are lucky. We've got it coming out of our ears. I think the government puts it in the water supply. Back in the U.S. of A. nothing helps a rooster rise to the top faster than a cocky attitude and a talent for taking the truth out for a night on the town. Take me, for example. I started out as a humble bird pecking at grit on a small farm in Kentucky.

Anyway, before the escape, the situation on the farm was grim. Troops need morale to perform under fire (my pal Fowler can tell you *all* about that, and then some...), and I could see that the girls needed a boost. I sent Nick and Fetcher off to rustle up a radio for a much-needed pick-me-up. Before you could say "Chick Berry," the girls were shaking their tail feathers and flapping to the beat. Even that old warhorse Fowler got in on the action. Next thing you know, Babs flapped a few times to keep from falling over and then *flew up onto the top bunk!* The gang went bananas. Flying—now that's a morale booster.

So there you have it: Rocky here transformed a morose gaggle of hens into a fine-tuned unit of escape chickens with just a little bit of good old American ingenuity. The party helped restore their confidence and believe in themselves once again. Plus, we had a blast. And therein lies the difference between Ginger's motivational philosophy and my own. Instead of scaring them silly, I pumped them up. You catch more bees with honey, after all, and it is a far more pleasant road to travel. Good ol' Rocky did his part to fill them with spirit, and the rest, as they say, is history.

—Rocky

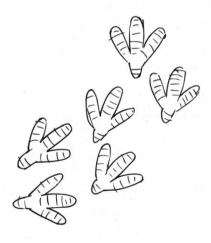

Mac's Inventions

Now that we dunnea have to worry about Mr. and Mrs. Farmer anymore, I have more time to work on some of me more creative inventions. Just look at these great new plans!

—Mac

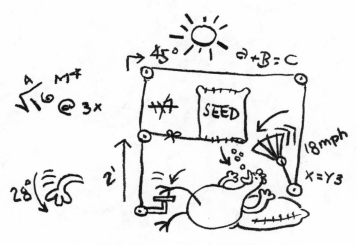

AIR CONDITIONER AND SELF-FEEDER

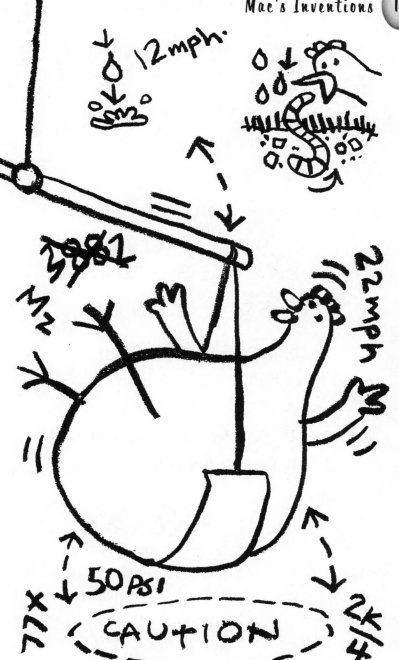

AUTOMATIC BIRDBATH

Fowler's Reflections

Volume One: Up from Sloth!
A Farm Rooster Joins the Service

"In my RAF days we were never allowed to waste time with unnecessary chitchat."

— FOWLER

Attention! You youngsters there—fall in line! The RAF didn't give you medals for acting like a bunch of hooligans. This is your lucky day. Fowler has decided to teach you all about the value of discipline. So sit down, and prepare to hear about my exploits in the Royal Air Force. These are not the stories your nanny might tell . . .

these are the kind that put feathers on your chest.

You see, back in my day, hens were hens, roosters were roosters, and the enemy we called Jerry was trying to take over the world. It was a grim time, full of danger and great fear. A cloud lay over England, and many brave chickens were beginning to despair. But they never expected the RAF! We were a proper squadron, we were. Not like you lot—always running around like a bunch of chickens with your heads . . . well, never mind that. WingCo (or Wing Command, for all you civvies out there) would give the order, and we would hop in the old crate and *chocks away!* We were off on yet another daring mission.

It was electrifying, and a jolly good time for all of us. We were lean and well-seasoned battle-fowl, nothing like the namby-pamby hothouse chickens of today. You young 'uns don't know how easy you have it. We birds of yesteryear hatched from a different kind of egg entirely. Eggs made of muscle and leather and filled with true grit. But the main difference between our generation and yours is that we had discipline! That is the most important quality a warrior can have going into battle. It doesn't matter if the battle is against Jerry or against a farmer . . . you must have it to succeed. We learned it in the Royal Air Force, and you youngsters will learn it from me. Whether you like it or not.

Let me start at the beginning. You there—stop that groaning! I was once a no-account wastrel, and you might be too if you don't pay attention here. I know that it may be difficult for you youngsters to believe, but I was wild and irresponsible once. I wanted to sleep all day and strut all night . . . just like your Uncle Rocky does. In my teenage years, I cruised the disreputable henhouses with my cronies, often **picking** fights with the young roosters from the other side of the farm. I was going nowhere fast, and I shudder to think what may have happened to me if things continued as they were. Yet at that time something wonderful happened: War broke out. Suddenly there was a demand for rough-and-tumble uneducated farm roosters. I abandoned my dream of playing the saxophone in low-rent juke joints and volunteered for the Royal Air Force. Little did I realize then how serious of a commitment I had made.

Okay, chicks . . . we must take a short break. I need my midmorning nap. We shall regroup at 1100 hours. In the meantime, ponder today's lesson: Discipline is the cornerstone of a warrior's strength. Though you don't believe it now, you need structure in order to grow up healthy and avoid the traps and pitfalls of adolescence. Company—dismissed!

—Wing Commander T. I. Fowler

Means of Escape

"So laying eggs all your life and then getting plucked, stuffed, and roasted is good enough for you, is it?"

— **GINGER**

In order to succeed in life it is important for a hen to set goals for herself. And I don't mean just meeting the daily egg quota. I firmly believe that one of the reasons that our escape from the farm was successful was because I buckled down and kept my eyes on the prize. I did not let the doubts of my fellow hens or the price-gouging practices of Nick and Fetcher interfere with my goal. While going through my journals, I uncovered this little piece I wrote about the longing to get away. I hope that it may help inspire you to escape from whatever personal prison you might find yourself a captive of. . . .

Every night I climb up onto the roof of this hut and gaze off at the distant hills. From up here it is easy to imagine a world without farmers, fences, and dogs. I close my eyes and think of a place where the grass is always green, the water clear and cool, and the worms are nice and fat. Bunty says the chances of getting out of here are a million to one. Even if she is right, then there is still a chance. That's what matters. And when I look out into the setting sun, and see the lush hilltops beckoning from a beautiful place not too far away, a fire rises within me and I feel up to the task of setting us free.

But then I turn my gaze back upon the dull brown of Tweedy's Farm, and my eyes are stung by the barbed fences and patrolling dogs. Hope fades in my chest. The only thing bright and fair in the farm is my dear flock of friends. And though I love them to death, what weapons do they offer to aid our escape? Bunty is so fat she bungles our escape plans. Babs is daft as taffy and can hardly remember her name. Oh, what hope does this bunch of misfits have against such a cruel enemy? What chance do we have against such a pitiless foe? Yet all these hens have put their faith and trust in me, and I cannot let them down. But the appointed task is so hard. So very, very hard.

Then I raise my eyes again, and look back over the hills. God helps hens who help themselves, I think. I must put my faith in myself. I know that the strength to fight comes from deep inside me, not from the imaginary rooster of my prayers. These hens are counting on me to lead them to freedom, and I will bust us out of here even if it kills me. Or puts me on the supper table, though I suppose the two are not mutually exclusive. Though the road seems long and dark, and unknown perils lie between us and our goals, I am not afraid to tread there. With God as my witness, we shall never be egg-layers again!

—Ginger

Everything You Need Is Right under Your Beak

Do you gals know what I see when I look around the room here? I see an amazing flock of beautiful chicks. And y'all are not just bits of feather and fluff, either. You've got brains: Look at Mac over there. You've got brawn: Bunty could pull the ears off of those dogs if she had the mind to do so. Or the confidence. And therein lies the problem, for that is the one thing I don't see yet in this room: confidence. But old Rocky here is gonna change that, because that's the one thing we are gonna need to pull us all together.

Every single one of you girls has potential, but most of you just don't believe in yourselves . . . yet. And who can blame you? You've had a tough life here. So far you've done a pretty good job of hatching your plans without getting caught. But there have been a few close shaves. Lucky for you Mr. Tweedy is dumb as a box of hammers. But that wife of his is another story. She's a heck of a lot smarter and a hundred times as mean. Then those dogs are lurking about. And on top of all these snoops, you've got to lay eggs *every day* to keep yourselves from becoming the *dish du jour*. Yikes! But here is the good news: Once you discover the strength you have inside, you'll realize that getting out of here is an egg you can crack.

Let me tell you a quick story about a certain young red-blooded American rooster. He was hatched in the great state of Kentucky. He didn't have much growing up, but he had a mama that believed in him . . . just like I believe in you gals now. So for her birthday he decided to sing her a song. It was just a little gift for someone who loved him, nothing more. But this is what happened: *He got discovered.* Ladies, that rooster was me.

This wacky fat man called the Colonel plucked me from obscurity and thrust me into the limelight. Well, soon I was singing bigger and bigger gigs and gaining more and more confidence. Then there was a change of plans, and I had to scramble before Mr. Herbs 'n' Spices served me up with a side of collard greens. But when I fled I took my confidence with me, and realized then that

Confidence was one thing that nobody could ever take away from me. *Ever.*

Now what I want from all of you is for each of you to give me a gift . . . only I don't want a song. I want each of you to do whatever it is you do best. Bunty, I want you to lay eggs like never before. Lay them with a vengeance; lay them for me. Mac, I want you to do some calculating and figure out this thrust thing you keep going on about. Babs, I want you to knit me a black turtleneck. I always thought I would look good in a black turtleneck. And Ginger . . . you've got the toughest assignment. I want you to continue to be the leader you are, and never give in. All these lovely ladies (and one cranky old rooster) need you more than you can imagine.

The Rock has spoken. Go on now and do what you do best. I know you can; I believe in all of you. One way or another, we're gonna fly this coop. Each of you has a gift: Use it! Now, which one of you has the Gift of Massage? Rocky could really use one. Being a motivational speaker isn't all grits and gravy, you know.

—Rocky

Fowler's Reflections

Volume Two: The Transformation of Young Mr. Fowler, Slacker

Gather round, young chicks, and shake those bits of eggshell out of your ears. Fowler shall now tell you . . . Hey, you, come back here and have a seat. . . . Where was I? Oh, yes. The story of my life. You chicks wouldn't be here if it weren't for me. You'd still be back on that horrible chicken farm instead of living it up out here in the fresh air. . . . Hello there, young sir! Where are you sneaking off to? Show a little more respect for your elders, you whippersnapper.

When I joined the service, I was a cocky young rooster with little regard for structure or discipline. My father had tried to instill such values in me, but had met with little success. Now it was the military's turn, and I would soon learn them in double time.

Boot camp was a shock. You chicks have it easy here, what with your nice warm nests and doting hens offering you whatever you want. Poppycock! It wasn't like that in the service, let me tell you. In one fell swoop my cozy little world vanished in a puff of gray smoke . . . replaced by a grim routine of forced marches and cold rations. Our drill instructor, Sergeant Krull, did his darnedest to constantly remind each of us roosters that we no longer lived under Mama Hen's wing. We ran ten miles in the snow each morning, uphill both ways. For breakfast we had a plate of cold worms, with no seconds. Lunch was cold worms, with a side of dirt. And for dinner . . . you guessed it . . . extra-cold worms.

Each day it got worse and worse, until one morning this fat young country rooster named Grimmy broke down in tears and blubbered that he couldn't take it anymore. Well, that was what Krull had been waiting for. He made an example out of that poor fellow. I won't dirty your young ears by telling you what happened then. Suffice to say that it motivated the rest of us birds not to show any weakness . . . ever. It was a rooster's idea of a living heck.

The awful food, the vermin-infested roosts, the forced marches with dogs, and screaming every morning . . . all these things were beginning to take their toll on Young Fowler, strong though I was. Luckily, I made some friends in boot camp, which helped ease the suffering. My favorite mate was a lanky rooster named Jocko. We helped each other through the more difficult obstacles, and that helped me begin to understand the value of teamwork and camaraderie. But even with the help of my mates, training was extraordinarily difficult. You chicks today whine and peep if you have to take out the trash. . . . Bah. You're all mollycoddled.

On the morning of my graduation I preened my dress-feathers and peeped into my looking glass. I was no longer Fowler, the undisciplined youth from the farm. I had become Wing Commander T. I. Fowler, RAF Mascot and Thunder-Rooster. Discipline, Order, and Precision were my watchwords now. The world was my henhouse, and I was ready for war.

Okay, hatchlings . . . time has come for my afternoon nap. Hello there, Missy, wake up. I said my nap, not yours! Pip pip. Before we disband, I will give you an order. You are to think about what I have told you, and apply my lessons to your own directionless lives. All of you lack discipline, but that can change. You see now that it can lead to salvation! Company, fall out. . . .

—Wing Commander T. I. Fowler

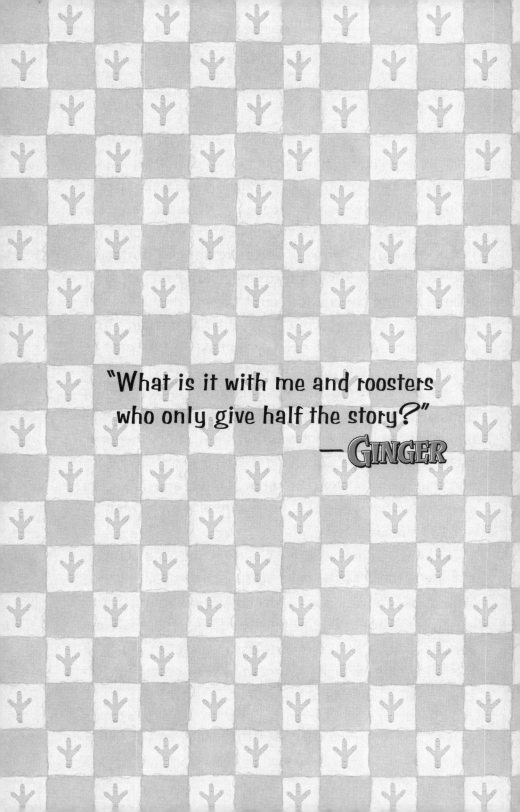

"What is it with me and roosters
who only give half the story?"
—GINGER

Section Two

BETWEEN A FLOCK AND A HARD PLACE:

On Friends and Family

A Letter to My Kin

"Stupid, worthless creatures. I'm sick and tired of making minuscule profits."
— Mrs. Tweedy

Dear Offspring,

I am writing this letter to you, my future nieces and nephews, so you may never suffer my fate. Nobody likes to be poor, but there are even worse things: You could be trapped on a chicken-infested farm with an oafish dolt for a husband. Such is the way my life has unfolded, and I don't want you to fall prey to such a cruel doom.

Therefore, I have outlined a foolproof moneymaking scheme designed to keep you in <u>chocolate</u> and silk forever. All that I ask is that a substantial percentage be put toward my retirement and that you provide all the start-up capital. Enclosed you will find a contract outlining the terms of the agreement. If you have any questions, I refer you to my lawyer . . . you ungrateful whelp. Here is the plan:

Gather up about one thousand plump young turkeys. The key to this endeavor is volume. Volume in more ways than one, as you shall soon see. Next, have your nit of a husband construct your turkey shacks right next to your neighbor's lodgings. Be sure to keep *your* home as far from the fowl gobblers as possible. Stock the turkey hovels with the turkeys. Now chickens (loathsome as they are) are not very noisy. You get a bit o' clucking here and there, and if you've got a rooster he'll do some crowing, but that's about it. Turkeys, on the other hand, rend the skies with the most unearthly gobbling noises you've ever heard. This is why you plant them next to your neighbors. The resulting fracas will wind them up in two ticks of the clock. Soon they'll be forced to sell, and you can gobble up (sorry) their land and move on to the next neighbor. As you work your way across the countryside you will soon become a wealthy land baron, and your dear old mother will finally have the wealth she has always deserved.

There will of course be legal issues at the onset of your turkey offensive, but this is why you have lawyers.

Your neighbors will initially complain, and you shall claim you are a turkey farmer and it is your state-given right to keep and bear birds, no matter how noisy. If your neighbors dig in their heels and refuse to budge, lean on the turkeys. I've come up with several methods of increasing the overall gobbling yield. Begin with the tried and true . . . withholding feed until their shrieks reach the proper intensity. It is important here to provide plenty of water so their wattles do not dry out. Water is cheap and feed is not. Keep this in mind. In fact, this may prove a cost-efficient course of action whether you have problems with your neighbors or not.

A more extreme, but no less effective, method of increasing noise production is to electrify the birdbaths. That way, your neighbors will be subjected to intermittent hair-raising shrieks whenever some gormless turkey dips his scrawny neck into the water. Imagine: The power flickers out because of a short circuit, and your neighbors are trapped out there in the dark while all about them the very air itself is rent with 'orrible screeches. They'll be out in no time!

There you have it. In no time you will preside over an empire of abandoned farmland. Although your name will be cursed throughout the countryside, I expect you will find this none to difficult a cross to bear. After all, you now *own* the countryside! And in case you are wonder-

ing what to do with your multiple flocks of distraught
Tom turkeys, I have a single word to whisper in your ears.
There is a wonderful American custom that will solve this
little problem. And the name of that magical, wonderful,
liquidating custom is . . . Thanksgiving.

—Mrs. Tweedy

What Am I Supposed to Do Now?

"There's a better place out there—some-where beyond that hill. . . ."

— GINGER

Well, we've done it. We've finally gotten to a better place. A place with trees and green grass and a discernible lack of farmers wielding pie-making contraptions. We are all safe here. Our efforts have paid off and my hopes and dreams have been answered. There is only one problem: What am I supposed to do now?

I've spent the last few years of my life plotting and scheming up ways to get us out of that grotty farm. I've spent every waking moment thinking up elaborate plans, negotiating with rodentia for black-market merchandise, and rallying the girls with inspirational slogans. Slogans like "The fences aren't just round the farm. They're up here—in your heads!" They were good slogans. But now that we don't need slogans anymore, I don't know what to do. Leading revolutions is the only thing I've done for so long. I can't just turn it off like a switch. I need a mission!

I think my attitude is starting to upset my friends. Just yesterday Babs asked me if I had seen her knitting needles. I told her, "That's the problem with you: You're daft as a biscuit. You can't remember anything. The needles are not lost. They're up here—in your head!" Well, she just sort of clucked at me in a concerned manner and wondered if maybe it was time for me to go on another holiday. She pointed out that I hadn't had one since we were back on the farm. Then she asked me if I had seen her needles again.

Rocky thinks I need to learn how to relax. He told me he was a master of the art, and he would be glad to teach me. But relaxing just doesn't feel right. I need to be *doing* something—preferably for a cause.

Mac suggested I pursue a degree in political science, and recommended a correspondence course with a nearby university. She said that it would be easier that way, what with me being a chicken and all. But I'm not sure if I am university material, so I'm going to put that on the back burner.

It was Nick and Fetcher of all people who actually had the most intriguing idea. They told me I should write a screenplay about our adventures. They said they knew some Hollywood producers (God only knows how, but somehow I'm not surprised) and could get me an audience. They are going to make some calls, and in the meantime they told me to work on my pitch. It's a long shot, but more impossible things have happened around this place. Maybe if we all work together. . . .

—Ginger

Pack Rats Are People, Too

NICK: We're the blokes that can make things happen.

FETCHER: And disappear.

NICK: That's right. We're a regular pair of magicians. Conjurors, if you will.

FETCHER: Full of deep knowledge. And deep pockets.

NICK: As I was saying, we make things happen. Escape planning is all well and good, but a proper plan requires proper equipment.

FETCHER: That's where we come in!

NICK: These birds would never have made it off the farm without us rats. Ya see, most folks look down upon us. They don't see talent . . . they see pests. But it is hustlers like us who make the impossible possible. Or at least affordable. We're the movers and shakers. We put the merchandise on the table.

FETCHER: And sometimes we take it off.

NICK: Hush up, you. Ginger used to regard us as common thieflike rodents. She always kept us at wing's length. Not that she wasn't fair—she always paid up front. Not like that canny Yank she fell in with.

FETCHER: Hang on . . . Rocky's a mate.

NICK: Aye. But he's no saint. At the start of all this he tried to play us. Imagine . . . him trying to pass off a story about roosters layin' eggs.

FETCHER: *You* bought it.

NICK: He was a smooth talker. But you are distracting me from my main point. See, Ginger warmed up to us once she saw that we were not bad eggs . . . just opportunistic.

FETCHER: Mmmm . . . eggs . . .

NICK: That's enough, hungry. What I am trying to convey is that, before the great escape, we was stuck in this demeaning relationship with the chickens on the farm. We were scavengers, and they was egg-layin', tax payin' establishment birds. And then in dropped the Yank, and he shook up the social order. He was the first bloke to recognize our talent for what it was.

FETCHER: I believe he called us "the sneakiest, most light-fingered, thieving parasites that he'd ever met."

NICK: Gets you right here, don't it? And later on, when he

chickened out, who did the birds come to for help?

FETCHER: Us rats!

NICK: Before Rocky came, we couldn't weasel a single egg out of them hens. Next thing you know, they're practically throwing 'em at us! That made us happy. And happy scavengers are good scavengers. Because of our efforts, Ginger and company was able to build the crate which took us all to the promised land. Now we are heroes! We helped save them all . . . and we got the chance to show our mettle because someone believed in us.

FETCHER: That's the moral, then.

NICK: There it is. Just give someone a chance to show you what they can do. They just might surprise you.

FETCHER: Well put, partner. Now let's go find us a snack.

NICK: Agreed. Bunty laid three fat ones today. Now here's the plan. . . . You distract her by throwing this rock at her, and while she roughs you up I'll make off with the goods.

FETCHER: Why do I always have to get beat up on?

NICK: Because you're so good at it.

Rocky's Confession

"You know, you're the first chick I ever met with the shell still on."

—ROCKY

There are hens, and then there are hens. And then there is Ginger. She's enough to drive a rooster to madness, or at least make him fly the coop.

I guess I didn't have much experience with strong-willed, idealistic gals before I met this crew. I used to be in showbiz; I was used to prima donnas and flakes. Don't even get me started on circus hens. They've got serious issues. They're in the circus for a reason, you know. One minute they think you're the cock of the walk, and the next you're yesterday's news. But with them it's not like you get mad because you can't figure them out, you just can't figure them out because there is nothing there. Just sultry black eyes and a lot of fluff.

Ginger is different; Ginger has substance. She's a gal that has pluck, and will never get plucked, if you catch my drift. She's tough. She's also the most hard-boiled egg old Rocky here has ever had to crack. For you see, your average hen is rendered helpless upon prolonged exposure to the Rock's raffish charms. I'd put myself at about SPF 20 (Serious Plumage Factor). I will not lie to you, folks. Their feathers tremble. They swoon. They compliment my tuckus. But Ginger, well, one of the first moves she pulled on me was blackmail. ME! BLACKMAIL! ON ME! Imagine . . . just at the moment I needed her most, she threatened to throw me to the dogs. Does that chick have spunk, or what? Well, in order to preserve my beak I agreed to help her, of course. I was just buying myself a bit of time to figure a way out of that mess. I needed a place to lay low. Plus the gals at the farm really knew how to welcome a fellow.

I was treated like a king from day one. I was pampered, massaged, and coddled by all the hens until I could barely say "more." Except for Ginger. She was just so demanding. She kept insisting on "status reports" and complaining about the "lack of progress." She just wouldn't let up. I thought she was a feathered slave driver with a secret rooster-bashing agenda. But that was before I got to know how good her heart was, and how much I failed to know my own.

And the more I got to know Ginger, the more guilty I began to feel about our "misunderstanding" . . . i.e., the fact that I couldn't fly any more than a fish could country line-dance. So what was I to do? After they found out my wing was healed, I did the only thing I knew how to . . . I ran away.

Alone with my thoughts, I was forced to contemplate my cowardly ways. I saw that for the first time in my life I had something real and something good. And I threw it away because I was too chicken (pardon please) to level with them. I got to thinking that Ginger would never have done such a thing. She would never have run away and left her friends in need. I knew right then that I had to go back. And the strength I needed to make my decision came from Ginger.

It turned out all right for old Rocky in the end, and for Ginger and all the others as well. Especially well for Ginger . . . at least I think. You see, I fell beak over tail feathers in love with Ginger. I'm a whole new rooster now, and it's all because Ginger demonstrated the character to show me the way.

—Rocky

I Remember Edwina

"What about Edwina? Did she die in vain?"

— GINGER

Back on Tweedy's Farm there was a hen of whom I was particularly fond. Her name was Edwina, and she was always there to lend a wing. Unfortunately, one dark day Mrs. Farmer served her for dinner because she had failed to lay an egg.

I blamed myself for the loss of dear Edwina. I felt that it was I who had failed. You see, this tragedy occurred at a time when I was planning our escape from the farm. As hens, our role on the farm was that of egg-producing machinery. We were not thought of as creatures with thoughts and feelings, to them we were simply profit-generating robots. If one of us failed to lay an egg, she would end up in the pot. It was an awful day-to-day existence, and I tremble even now just thinking about it.

Not all of us hens (with the exception of dear Bunty) could lay eggs every night like clockwork. Some nights I might lay two eggs, while the next night I would fail to lay even one. So whenever one of us did not produce an egg, another hen would give her an extra. I tried my best to keep tabs on the egg-distribution, but the responsibility of escape planning demanded much of my time. Sadly, I failed to ask Edwina if she needed an egg on that fateful day. So even though there were enough to go around, I didn't get one to Edwina when she needed it the most. Stupid, stupid Ginger! How could I have been so negligent?

All the other hens said that it was not my fault that Edwina got stuffed and roasted. "After all," they told me, "you can't do everything for everybody. Edwina knew she didn't have an egg, so she should have done something about it herself. She knew she could have gone to Bunty, but she probably froze up. You know how scary egg call was. So stop blaming yourself, Ginger."

But I couldn't stop. After Edwina was taken, I doubled my efforts to find a way out. Her untimely demise served to increase the pressure I put on myself to try and come up with a perfect plan. I told myself that I must find a means of escape. That way, I thought, Edwina will not have died in vain. And in the end, we did make it out. Against all odds we found a way.

Yet even after we gained our freedom, I could not stop thinking about her. Then one night, as I lay on my back on top of my favorite hill, something strange happened. I heard a voice far off in the distance, a voice that seemed somehow very familiar to me. With a shock, I realized that it belonged to Edwina. Suddenly, an enormous chicken-shaped thunderhead rose up from a bank of clouds before me.

"Braak," the voice began, "Ginger Hen, it is I . . . Edwina the Chicken."

"But, how is this possible?" I stammered.

"Oh, it is possible, dear. Do you not see me before you? All things are possible, luv."

"But you were roasted by the cruel farmers. They took you away because you didn't lay an egg. I know what I saw."

"Then tell me what you see now, child."

"I see the beloved beak and eyes of my dear friend Edwina, whose goose was cooked back on the farm. But I do not understand how . . ."

"Silence! I do not have much time. Pulling off this giant-head-in-the-clouds trick is impressive, but tiring. I have not come to explain myself. Rather, I have come to give you peace. You have carried the guilt of my doom for too long. It is time to let go, Ginger."

I began to weep. "I feel so bad. I was trying to save us all, and yet I lost you."

"Look around you, hen. You *have* saved us all. Without you the others would not be free, and I would not get to pull off these awe-inspiring cloud tricks. And I like them. So let me go, Ginger, and live in peace."

Suddenly I awoke. I was lying out on a hilltop underneath the stars, and my heart was beating like mad. There was a small dribble of drool coming out of a corner of my beak. I had been dreaming. Yet I felt different than I did before I went to sleep. I felt at peace.

I have never told anyone else about this strange dream . . . until now. Maybe this tale will help others who have, like me, blamed themselves for the slow-roasting of a dear friend who failed to lay an egg on schedule. Heaven knows they should not carry their guilt around forever, as I almost did. I ask these people to heed the words of Edwina and to "let go." I did, and it has made all the difference. Sometimes someone has to get eaten so that the others may survive.

—Ginger

Thoughts from a Hen in Solitary Confinement

"I wasn't on holiday, Babs."—GINGER

Back on the farm I spent quite a bit of time in Mr. Farmer's coal-bunker. Not by choice, of course . . . it was his way of punishing me for trying to escape. Well, a girl can't help but do a bit of thinking in a situation like that. I thought about my friends and what they meant to me, and it was these thoughts that gave me strength to try again.

Babs, you dear sweet thing. Though you are daft as a post, you have a gentle heart. Each time you ask me about my "holiday," I just can't bring myself to tell you where I've been. Last time you asked me if I enjoyed my spell in St. Tropez. You asked me if beaches are really as sandy as people say, and you wondered if chickens can get a suntan. Where *do* you get these thoughts? I wonder if maybe you scratched your head with your needles one day and accidentally poked yourself in the brain. I thanked you for the bathing cap you knitted for me, though all I really use it for is to keep my head warm during these cold nights underground.

And good old Bunty . . . even though you are not fully convinced about the need to escape, you still pitch in with your eggs. You really are a marvel; I often wonder how a hen can possibly lay as many as you do. Sure, you can be a bit gruff at times, but you've got it where it counts.

I get so lonely down here that I even start to miss your stories from the war, Fowler, and if nothing else that should help you understand how utterly bleak and desolate a place this is. One time in the hole I realized that it was Tuesday, and I would be missing your lecture. Suddenly it didn't seem so bad anymore. That more than anything got me through the night. Thank you, Fowler, thank you!

And where would we be without your brains, Mac? Well, ideally not on this farm, but we're working on that. I know that someday soon you'll hatch a brilliant scheme that might not even scorch, maim, sting, cripple, bruise, or mangle a single one of us. Oh dear, oh dear . . . forgive me, Mac, it is the solitude talking. I know that you'll get us out of this horrible farm. And in one piece, too.

I guess what I'm trying to say is this: You've got to stand by your flock. We're all in this together, and we'll all get out of it together. I have no doubts myself, but I do have one question: How come *I'm* the only one who gets locked up down here in this dratted cellar?

—Ginger

NICK: "Imagine a world before chickens—a chickenless, eggless world. Imagine that if you will."

FETCHER: "I am—and it's horrible."

Section
Three

**CHICKEN
NUGGETS:**
Choice Bits
of Eclectic
Wisdom

Mrs. Tweedy's Amazing List

One fine day Fetcher and I were shopping around in Mrs. Farmer's underwear drawer. We was looking for some merchandise, as always, but were surprised at what we found. Tucked in there among her bloomers and knickers and coupons for Wellington boots was a list! It turns out that Mrs. Farmer has hopes and dreams just like a normal person does after all. This is what we found:

1. Learn how to box
2. Tell children that they can't have any more birthdays
3. Take pleasure in the little things, such as diamonds
4. Cage an animal and exploit it for profit
5. Make a living off of the domination of weaker creatures
6. Take no joy in the simple pleasures of life

7. Marry a man easily cowed

8. Cow the man unmercifully

9. Wish for a life beyond my means

10. Regret chances I never took

11. Train attack dogs

12. Break into full-scale automated production

13. Hate my neighbors and never ever help them out

14. Breed a chicken that lays ten eggs a day, eats dirt, and cannot cluck

15. Chop off a chicken's head just for the sheer pleasure of it

16. Practice random acts of violence and senseless cruelty

17. Bully a bank manager

18. Bully some children

19. Take candy from a baby

20. Pull the wings off a fly

21. Pull the wings off a chicken

22. Dig into some chicken wings

23. Engage in arms trading

24. Roll a drunk

25. Fire an employee for no reason

26. Make a little girl cry

27. Turn all the chickens into profit-making pastry

The Rules for Being a Pack Rat

"Ask and ye shall receive." —

1. **You will need a partner.**
   Preferably one who is daft as a nit and easily manipulated . . . er . . . compensated. Right, Fetch?

2. **A proper business needs a plan.**
   Plan on doing a lot of slinking around at night and keeping odd hours.

3. **There is no such thing as stupid mistakes, only stupid partners.**
   My associate Fetcher, alas, is a proper example of such a nancy. It is not really his fault he is so dim; his mother thunked him on the head as a child.

4. **You must learn the art of scavenging.**
   Scavenging is an art, and good scavengers are proper

artists. The most important thing to remember is that *true* scavenging comes from within . . . from within houses, lorries, cabinets . . .

5. **Humans will want to bop you with hammers and such.**
   We do not like this, but it happens. The best way to prevent this is to pinch the hammer.

6. **A pack rat cannot live on chicken feed alone.**
   That is why we want nice, tasty eggs. The chickens don't want to give 'em up, though, so if you are to succeed, you must find the proper merchandise to part a hen from her booty.

7. **There is no such thing as stealing, only "sharing."**
   And it is important to share. Me mum taught me that.

8. **Some people may take issue with your chosen profession.**
   For whatever reason, humans seem curiously attached to their belongings. When blokes such as ourselves attempt to unattach them, they become upset (see *hammer*, above). Still, it's a living.

9. **Dogs are bad things.**
   In general, dogs oppose our humble efforts of acquisition. They howl, bark, and bite . . . and are generally unpleasant to be around. When this happens, see rule number 15.

10. **If at first you don't succeed, try and pinch again.**
    Sometimes it takes more than one try to acquire the goods. When this happens, a distraction often comes in handy. Have some fool make a noise to divert Farmer's attention (see *partner*, above).

11. **Necessity is the mother of borrowing.**
    And she is a cruel mother, always demanding that you borrow more and more.

12. **Scavenging is its own reward.**
    Me dear old mum told me that herself. She was a wise one, she was. Full of wonderful advice.

13. **Filching is a virtue.**
    In today's hectic world, it is important to have good values. Or was that "good value"?

14. **It is better to go in with a whimper than a bang.**
    That way, you won't get caught.

15. **It is not whether you can outrun the farmers, it is whether you can outrun your partner.**
    So be sure to keep fit, and pick a slow partner.

16. **Friends help you move. Real friends help you move merchandise.**
    'Nuff said.

—Nick the Pack Rat, Esq.

Decisions

A robust hen laid two eggs in a nice warm nest.

The first egg said, "Crikey, I can't wait to hatch. I'm growing and growing and there is hardly enough room in here for me anymore. Can you think about how great it will be when we get out of these shells and see what the world outside looks like? Surely there are all sorts of exciting things out there. I can't really begin to imagine what they might look like. I've just got to get out there and see what the world has to offer."

And with that the first baby chick pecked away at her egg, and, sure enough, soon her head poked through the crusty white shell and into her bright new world. "Right-O," she peeped, "this is really quite nice. You should come on out and have a peek."

But the second egg said, "No way, lassie. I'm a-staying right here in my egg. It is cozy and toasty-warm. You go on ahead and break up the only thing you know, the only world we understand. I'll stay back here where it is safe. Who knows what kinds of horrors might be out there? Not me. And I don't want to find out. You go on and I'll hold down the fort here in my shell. And don't say I didn't warn you. Cheerio."

So while the hatchling toddled about outside her nest investigating her new world, a bold pack rat slunk into the nest and made off with the reticent egg. "Can't believe my luck, this," he smiled, smacking his thin lips at the thought of his newfound prize. "This'll make me a smash-up meal with some bangers and chips."

MORAL OF THE STORY:
If you aren't moving ahead, you are falling behind. Worse, you may get gobbled up by a rat.

All I Ever Really Needed to Know I Learned at Tweedy's Farm

Now that we live in chicken paradise, we have the luxury of time. Time to talk, time to study the world around us, and time to reflect on the meaning in our lives. But the interesting thing is that despite the learning and life experience we've had since our escape, all that I ever needed to know I learned back on Tweedy's Farm.

Oh, by now you know what a horrible place it was, what with the barking dogs, cruel farmers, and prison-like living conditions. Nevertheless, it taught me so many important things: Share your eggs. Keep a stiff upper beak. Keep your nestbox clean. Playtime is important, especially dances. Keep an eye peeled for farmers. Don't talk with a mouthful of chicken feed. Keep your belongings in order—others share your henhouse, too. Have a nap (this especially applies to Fowler). Compliment a friend's knitting. Thank someone if she lends you an egg. Don't taunt the dogs. Sometimes it means a lot to listen to an old rooster's stories. Don't accept credit extensions from pack rats: The interest rate is too high. Try and understand things from another's point of view. In helping your friends, you help yourself. Appreciate what others do for you and thank them for it. Be a good egg.

So as we continue to lead our lives out here in our beautiful new home, all we need to do to keep things in proper order is live by the same lessons we learned back in our days on the farm. In spite of the hardships and (toward the end) the threat of being mechanically rendered into a pie, we learned to survive. More important, we learned to take care of each other and all get along. God only knows . . . with this group it isn't always easy.

—Ginger

The Value of a Puppy

Gather round, my nieces, and Auntie Melisha shall tell you a story about a little girl and her puppy. For you see, young Chrissy wants a puppy for her birthday. She did not ask for money or jewelry or anything practical . . . she simply asked me for a pet. Your sister has a problem that will get her into trouble one day unless she fixes it: Her value system is out of balance. Maybe this story will set her on the right path and help her to understand the true value of a puppy.

When I was a young girl my father bought me a puppy for my birthday—it was hairy and sort of brownish and it had a tail. I had not asked for it. Instead, I had asked my parents for a solid gold telly. My mother was pleased with my choice, but my father disagreed. "Look here," her told her, "a young girl should have a puppy.

Girls love puppies, and maybe it will help her open up and get along with the other children."

My mother disagreed. "Even though you can't afford a new telly on your salary, she is thinking along the right lines," she scolded. "Gold and jewels are what little girls should want. I am worried that you are confusing her with all this nonsense about pets and friends. I've been trying to teach her real, practical values her whole life, and here you come blundering along and toss a puppy into the gears. I can only hope my lessons have been well learned and you don't bugger everything up. As usual."

On the morning of my birthday my father called me. "Melisha," he said, "look what I have brought you. Soon you will know of the love and joy which comes from animal companionship."

"What does it do?" I asked, suspiciously poking at it with my big toe.

"Do? Why, it's a puppy! You can play with him and train him, and soon he will learn to fetch and come when you call. . . ."

"How much is it worth? In pounds sterling?"

"Look, Melisha, you're missing the point. This is about friendship. Stop thinking about money, darling, and open your heart. Here," he said, dangling the wretched creature in front of my nose. "See how he wiggles and wags his tail? That means he likes you!"

I scrunched my eyes together and peered sharply at the animal, then grasped its snout with my hand. In spite of my suspicion, I must admit I was a bit curious about this thing my father was giving me.

"This . . . puppy . . . is it from Harrods?"

"First off, luv, 'it' isn't an 'it.' 'It' is a 'he.' Second, this isn't like buying a lorry or motorcar. This is more like the way things are with people. The true value of a puppy is not measured in pounds. Do you understand what I am trying to say?"

I thought about it for a minute. "But isn't it better to be rich?"

"Money is a tool, Melisha. It doesn't make a person any better or worse. It is what you *do* with the money that matters. Spending your money on other people rather than yourself helps make you a good person."

"But I don't want to be a 'good' person. I want to be a *rich* person. I want to have money so I can buy more and more things that I will never use. That way, no one else can have them because I own them."

"You have been spending far too much time with your mother, lamb chop."

"She agrees with me. She says it is better to be rich and alone than to be poor and have friends. That's why it is okay that I don't have any friends . . . because one day I am going to be rich, rich, rich! And I am not sure how this puppy fits into my long-range plans."

"Just give him a chance, Melisha. Please?"

I agreed to use it for one week on a trial basis, satisfaction guaranteed or my money back. That is to say, if I did not fall in love with the puppy after a week, my dad would give me the money he paid for it. He was convinced that after a few days the fuzzy beast would wiggle its way into my heart.

A week later when I had my money, I went shopping alone for the first time in my life. I felt like a grown-up at last. I had a pocket full of dosh and could buy whatever I wanted. Oh, the freedom . . . the heady, heady freedom! As I wandered along the street, various trinkets caught my eye. For a while, I felt as though I would never find the perfect thing. But then I saw it. Bound in rich leather, with smooth, creamy pages just waiting to be filled with numbers. It was an accounting ledger, and I fell in love.

So you see, girls, if I had given in to my father and kept the puppy, I would never have found my first ledger. And without that, I never would have been able to track my finances the way I have. And isn't that much better—and more profitable—than a nasty little flea-catcher? Of course it is!

I hope this little story has helped you all. There there, Chrissy, don't cry. Auntie Melisha has something else for your birthday. Something nice! Look . . . a shiny new penny! Just give it back to me (I'll take that back, dear . . . thank you very much) and I'll invest it, and next year . . . if you are lucky and this bull market holds . . . you'll have *two* shiny new pennies. Soon it shall grow into enough for you to track in your own account book. Thanks to Auntie Melisha, you've now learned the true value of a puppy.

—Mrs. Tweedy

Them Treacherous Birds,

or
What I Have Learned from My Chickens

"I told you they was organized."
—MR.TWEEDY

I may not know much, but one thing I do know is chickens. The Tweedy clan has been raising chickens for as long as ye can remember. Chicken is in our blood, so to speak. I've got a sharp eye when it comes to those dodgy beasts, and I saw that they was up no good right quick. The missus didn't believe me. Not at first, anyway. She said 'twas all in me head, though she told me she was surprised there was room for it up there. But I knew better. I knew they was up to summat.

I saw 'em up and around at odd times. They was nosing about and doing strange things. They was plotting and scheming and operating heavy machinery. Them chickens are smarter than they look, you know. That's their disguise. They lull a person into a false sense of security then . . . WHAM! Their trap crashes down upon you. A man cannot spend his entire existence around a pack of deceptive fowl without learning a few of their habits, eh? Oh, I know them well.

These chickens . . . they're wily. Keen of wit and sharp of beak. When they attack, they gang up on you. Peck at your eyes. A single man, well, he can put down a chicken in a fair fight. But ten chickens? Twenty? That's how they operate, you see . . . like a pack of wild dogs. They're ruthless, with a kind of gang mentality. Like football fans, almost, but they're shrewd and cunning as well. 'Tis a deadly combination.

After I saw that they were up to no good, I took it upon myself to investigate further. Making me rounds, I lost my caution and walked into their lair . . . right smack through the front door! This was my one grievous mistake, and I paid dearly for it. What I saw inside boggled the imagination. They was building a bloody plane! CHICKENS! AERONAUTICAL ENGINEERING! Before I could so much as scream, they jumped me. Next thing I knew they was all over me . . . peckin' and a-scratchin' and cackling like the devil himself. I was outnumbered and terrified.

'Twas not the first time them chickens pulled one over on the Tweedy clan, neither. Back when I was but a young whelp on the farm, me pa told me about me Uncle Jimmy. Said he was done in by a chicken . . . a big strong brute rooster named Bucko. He caught my uncle coming home from the pub after a long night out. It was raining that evening, hard. My pa found Jimmy the next morning, facedown in a puddle by the side of the road. Bucko had lifted his wallet to make it look like a robbery. Nobody could prove it for certain, but it has been handed down as truth. Bucko ended up in a casserole the following night, but nothing my pa could do would ever bring me uncle back.

I've learned many a thing in my life, yet I can boil every shred of it down to a few simple bits of advice. This is what I have learned from the chicken; pay attention for these tips might very well save your life one day:

- Give a chicken an inch, she'll take a yard.
- A lone chicken is no threat; a pack of chickens is a menace. They prefer to travel in packs.
- Behind every thieving garden gnome is a chicken with a plan.

- If they come at you, the best thing to do is roll into a ball to protect your vitals.
- Never ever, under any circumstances, turn your back on a chicken.

'Tis sound advice, but whenever I offer it to someone, they look at me as if I've gone bats. When I told my boys down at the pub about me Uncle Jimmy, they just laughed and laughed. 'Twas cruel laughter, too. Just like those chickens laugh, I reckon. . . . Truth be told, I'm deathly afraid of them now. I've said it before and I shall say it again: Never turn your back on a chicken. Chickens are a force to be reckoned with . . . raw, elemental, shot through with the chaos of nature. Engage them at your own peril, and God be with ye if you do.

—Mr. Tweedy

"Aw, shut up and dance!"

—BUNTY

WHAT MAKES ME HAPPY:
Soothing Balm for Troubled Souls

Why I Love Knitting

There is nothing I enjoy more than a good knit. It is the first thing I think of in the morning and the last thing I do before I tuck myself in at night. Morning knits are quite nice. I love waking up and grabbing my needles for a quickie before breakfast . . . it gets me going and puts a smile on my face for the rest of the day! Of course, the morning knit is just the first knit in a long day of knitting possibilities. Even when I'm not knitting, I'm thinking about it. I guess I've got knitting on the brain!

Back on the farm, knitting used to help calm me down. Sometimes the dogs would bark at me and make me quite nervous. Whenever that happened, out came the needles and the knitting began. My fears just melted away as my needles clacked together, slowly at first then growing faster and faster until POP! Out sprang a nice frock and I giggled and got a bit sleepy and relaxed for a spell. Nothing like a fine frock to soothe a chicken's soul!

Back then it was risky to knit in public. But that made it a bit more exciting. There was always the chance that Mr. Farmer would catch me, so I had to be sly. I would end up knitting in the strangest of places! Under a feeder, behind the henhouse, and even once in the boot of Mr. Farmer's motorcar—I've knitted in all these places! It doesn't even matter what I am knitting; I don't so much care about that. A jumper, a beak-warmer, knickers, a tea cozy . . . it could be anything. It is just the act of knitting that does it for me, you see.

Sure, I'm not like all the other girls. I know that I am different. But that is what makes me special! After all, a girl has to find what it is she truly fancies and do that thing well. With Bunty, laying eggs is what she is best at. Knitting is my gift. It makes me happy and complete. And with that, I'll be off . . . I feel the urge coming on, and I never could say no!

—Babs

These Are a Few of Me Favorite Things

What makes me happy? Hmm . . . 'tis an odd enough question. I like to sit down to a piping hot meal . . . preferably including chicken . . . and maybe a nice slice of apple pie with a spot o' ice cream on the side. Maybe some bangers and mash, or a bit of takeout from the chippie down the lane. Food makes me feel happy, and a kind word from the missus will make me feel good. I don't feel "good" often as I like, as the wife is none too free with her praise, but there is one other thing that makes me feel good: a chicken in a pen.

Seeing a fenced-up chicken makes me feel proper and in control. And that feeling I get when I eat a chicken is right proper, too. Especially if it was a chicken who was giving me sauce, or a chicken that was making me particularly nervous. Then the bird goes from giving me sauce to being *in* sauce, and once I eat 'em, I know that they won't make me nervous no more.

Knowing that the chickens are locked up in a hut makes me feel safe. Then I can rest easy, knowing that they can't come and get me when I'm sleeping. That's when they come, you know . . . at night. Out there in the dark, when you're all alone. Chickens is trouble. Can't take any chances with 'em.

But mostly I like a full tummy and a bit of a kip. I'll take in a pint down at the pub with my mates. They never call me a nit or a big pudding or any such things . . . at least not to my face. I can get all that here at home from the missus. She's so good with the hard words, it makes me wonder why she can't be quicker with the kind ones. Still, I do as she says as I want to make her happy. Because when she's happy, she's more likely to toss me a kind word. So I do as I can and hope for a bit of praise. She is my wife, after all, and I do me best. And I keep an eye on them birds.

—Mr. Tweedy

A Special Place

Since the day that I hatched, all I have ever heard about is how lovely our new home is and how lucky we are to live wild and free in the countryside. Even Babs—my own mother—says that our home is the grandest place in the whole wide world. She says that she doesn't even see the point of going on holiday, now that we live here in the best of all possible worlds.

But you know what makes my heart sing like nothing else? Thinking that maybe there is a better place out there somewhere. Someplace not too far away, either; it could be just beyond that hill over there. Oh, maybe I'm just crazy, but it makes me happy, and what if . . . just what if . . . I am right?

Imagine a place where we could all live together in a proper henhouse—a place where we each had our own cozy nestbox that we didn't have to share with anyone else. Imagine having a real wooden floor beneath our feet, none of this damp grass that is full of stickers and briars. Someplace safe and protected . . . maybe with a large fence around it to keep the bad animals out. There would be someone there to feed us every day so we wouldn't have to scratch for our own food all the time.

Oh . . . just the thought of waking up in a cozy wooden box every morning while someone pours lots of nice food into a trough makes me feel all giddy inside. We could get nice and fat, just like my Aunt Bunty.

Hmm . . . but what would we do for a living there? Nick and Fetcher tell me that eggs are quite valuable. . . . I know—we could lay eggs for a living! Why not? That's one thing us chickens know how to do quite well, and Aunty Bunty herself has told me it is a perfectly acceptable line of work. 'Twas her own mother's and her mother's mother's profession. Our days would be spent lolling about near the hut, peckin' at this and scratchin' at that, while we gossip and knit and take nice long naps whenever the mood strikes us. The cruel world would be kept out with our big, strong fence, and whenever the food in our bowls ran low, more would come a-pourin' in.

Wow, the very thought of it makes me woozy! Maybe such a place doesn't exist, but I believe it does. One day I'm going to get out of here and go look for it myself, when I grow a bit older and stronger. We won't live like this forever, I swear! I'm going to find this magical place. Maybe not today, maybe not tomorrow . . . but I will find it. I, Ally Hen, will lead us chickens to a better place!

—**Ally Hen**

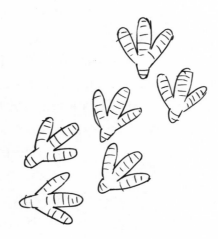